Rosie and Tortoise

Board of Education City of New York

Mayor's Classroom Library Initiative

For the adorable Maddie Bradley. M.W.
For Robyn Mathison, the Guardian Angel
of Mary Street. R.B.

DK Publishing, Inc.
95 Madison Avenue
New York, New York 10016

Visit us on the World Wide Web at http://www.dk.com

Library of Congress Cataloging-in-Publication Data

Wild, Margaret [date]
Rosie and Tortoise / by Margaret Wild ;
illustrated by Ron Brooks.
p. cm.
"A DK Ink book."
Summary: Rosie the hare is afraid to hold her
premature baby brother because he seems so
fragile—until their father tells her a special
story about a tortoise and a hare.
ISBN 0-7894-2630-7
[1. Hares—Fiction. 2. Babies—Fiction. 3. Brothers and sisters—Fiction.]
I. Brooks, Ron, ill. II. Title. III. Series.
PZ7.W64574Ro   1999   [E]—dc21 99-13445 CIP

Book design by Ron Brooks.
The illustrations for this book were done in pencil and watercolor.
The text of this book was hand-lettered by Ron Brooks.
Printed in Hong Kong.

First American Edition, 1999
10 9 8 7 6 5 4 3 2

Published in Australia by Allen & Unwin Pty Ltd.

Rosie and Tortoise

Story by Margaret Wild

Pictures by Ron Brooks

A DK INK BOOK
DK PUBLISHING, INC.

Rosie couldn't wait
for her baby brother to be born.

"I'll teach him how to hop,
leap,
and run–

just like me!" she told her mom.

"When is he going to be born, Mom? When?"

"Be patient," said Mom.
"It'll be a while yet."

But she was wrong.
Bobby was born the very next day.
He was the smallest,
weakest little hare ever.

"He only weighs as much as an onion!"
said Mom.

"We'll fatten him up," said Dad.

Rosie stared at her tiny brother.
He hardly even seemed to be breathing.
Suddenly she felt as scared as that time
she'd been chased by a fox.

"Would you like to hold him?" said Mom.

"No," said Rosie.

The days went past.

The family took Bobby out in the carriage
to give him some fresh air and sun.

"He's a bit bigger and a bit stronger," said Mom.

"He weighs as much as a potato now!" said Dad.

"Would you like to push the carriage, Rosie?"

"No," said Rosie. And she ran after a butterfly.

One morning Mom said,
"Bobby's nearly as heavy as a turnip!"

"It won't be long before he weighs as much as a cauliflower!" said Dad.

But Rosie thought that Bobby looked as sickly as ever. And when Mom asked her to come and rock the cradle, she said "No," and went off to play on the swing.

Later that day Rosie and Dad
went out picking blackberries.
"Rosie," said Dad, "why don't you like Bobby?"
Rosie nearly dropped her basket.
"I do!" she said. "It's just..."
She stopped,
then she whispered,
"He's so tiny,
it makes me scared."

"Come and sit next to me, Rosie," said Dad,
"I want to tell you a story."

"Once upon a time, there was a hare and
a tortoise who were best friends.
One day they went gathering nuts in

the forest, each going their own way,
but at going~home time Tortoise couldn't
find Hare anywhere, so he set off alone.

When night fell, he was still plodding on, saying to himself,

'Slow and steady does it, slow and steady will get me safely home.'

Little by little, Tortoise made his way
toward the edge of the forest, where

he saw what looked like a yellow moon moving through the trees.

And there, coming to meet him,

was Hare, with a lantern."

Rosie sat quietly, thinking.
When Bobby was born, he'd weighed the same
as an onion. Then a potato, then a turnip.

One of these days he would weigh as much
as a cauliflower, perhaps a cabbage,
even a pumpkin!

Rosie smiled.

"Bobby is slow and steady," she said. "Isn't he?"

"He is," said Dad.

That night
Rosie held her brother
for the first time.

She could feel
his heart beating against hers.

"Hey, Bobby," she said,
"hey there, little Tortoise!"